ATHENEUM, *New York* *1970*

A & THE

or

William T. C. Baumgarten Comes to Town

by

ELLEN RASKIN

This book is dedicated to everyone who can read **a** and **the.**

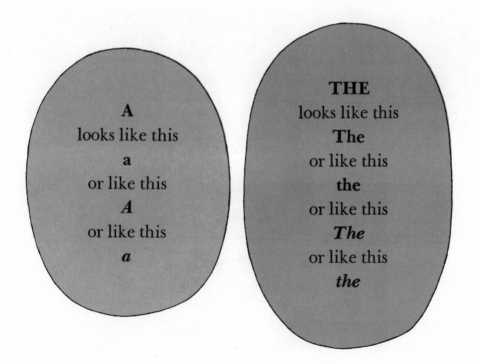

A
looks like this
a
or like this
A
or like this
a

THE
looks like this
The
or like this
the
or like this
The
or like this
the

The moving van pulled away from **the** house with **the** orange tree and drove off. **A** new family had moved to Thirteenth Street.

Thirteenth Street had two trees. One was **the** orange tree, which wasn't really an orange tree at all. That is, it didn't grow oranges. In fall its leaves turned **a** brilliant orange; it was called **the** orange tree to distinguish it from **the** other tree on **the** block, which had no leaves at any time, summer or fall. That tree was called **the** other tree.

The other tree stood before **the** apartment building where Horace and his sister Doris lived.

No tree grew in front of Morris' house, but there was **a** fire hydrant.

There was nothing at all in front of Luke's building, only sidewalk.

Horace, Doris, Morris and Luke lingered around **the** other tree, trying to catch **a** glimpse of their new neighbors.

Slowly **the** front door of **the** house with **the** orange tree opened. Horace, Doris, Morris and Luke ran to **the** fire hydrant to get **a** better look.

"I hope it's **a** girl my size," whispered Doris.

"I hope so, too," whispered Horace, tired of having his little sister tagging along.

The door opened wider. Horace, Doris, Morris and Luke ran to **the** orange tree. Out onto **the** stoop stepped **a** boy in **a** blue hat and **a** blue suit.

"I don't think I like him," whispered Morris.

"I don't think I like him, either," whispered Luke.

"Why not?" asked Doris.

"We just don't." Horace pulled Doris back behind **the** orange tree.

The new boy walked down the front steps and cautiously approached the staring group.

"I just moved in," said the new boy.

"That was a dumb thing to say," thought Horace.

"That's nice," replied Doris. "What's your name?"

"What's yours?" the new boy asked.

"We asked first," answered Morris.

"My name is Doris, and this is my brother, Horace. And this is Morris, and this is Luke."

"My name," the new boy said proudly, "is William T. C. Baumgarten."

"William T. C. Baumgarten?" giggled Horace.

"William T. C. Baumgarten?" tittered Morris.

"William T. C. Baumgarten?" laughed Luke.

"What does the T. stand for?" asked Doris.

"The T. stands for The," answered William T. C. Baumgarten.

"The!" exclaimed Horace.

"The!" exclaimed Morris.

"The!" exclaimed Luke.

"I never heard of a name like The," pouted Morris.

"No one can have a name like The," shouted Luke.

"We don't like liars." Horace dragged Doris away from the new boy.

"What does the C. stand for?" Doris called back, but William T. C. Baumgarten had already climbed the stairs and closed the door behind him.

The next afternoon Horace, Doris, Morris and Luke met at **the** other tree and decided to walk around **the** block. They didn't want to meet William T. C. Baumgarten until they had discussed **the** matter of his strange name.

Morris said, "My mother said she never heard of **a** name like **The**."

Horace said, "My mother said she never heard of **a** name like **The**, either."

"My mother said that, too," added Doris. Horace gave his sister **a** disgusted look.

"My mother said maybe **the The** is short for Theodore," said Luke.

"Let's ask him if **the The** stands for Theodore," suggested Doris.

Horace, Doris, Morris and Luke darted around **the** corner. There under **the** orange tree was William T. C. Baumgarten sitting on **a** black bicycle.

"I sure hope **The** stands for Theodore," mumbled Luke, who didn't own **a** black bicycle, or **a** bicycle of any color.

"Hi," called William T. C. Baumgarten.

Horace wasn't too sure he wanted to be friendly until he

had settled **the** big question. Standing at **the** fire hydrant he shouted, "Does **the** T. in your name stand for Theodore?"

"No," William T. C. Baumgarten shouted back. "I told you yesterday, T. stands for **The**. **The** and only **The**."

The three boys angrily stomped off, with Doris, as usual, trailing behind.

"What does **the** C. stand for?" called Doris.

But they were already under **the** other tree and too far off to hear **the** answer.

Monday morning Horace, Doris, Morris and Luke walked to school together.

"Do you think he will be in our class?" asked Horace as they crossed Twelfth Street.

"I hope not," Morris said.

"He's too stupid to be in our class," said Luke.

"I don't think so," said Doris.

They walked past **the** grocer neatly stacking fresh vegetables in **the** window.

"'Maybe T. stands for tomato," said Horace laughing.

They walked past **the** pharmacist unlocking **the** front door of **the** drug store.

"Maybe T. stands for toothpaste," said Morris.

They walked past **the** plumber arguing with **a** customer over **the** telephone.

"Maybe T. stands for toilet," gasped Luke.

The three boys laughed so hard all **the** way to school that no one heard Doris ask, "I wonder what **the** C. stands for."

Horace left Doris at **the** kindergarten door and **the** boys strolled down **the** hall to room 21 **A.** They were seated only **a** minute when in walked **the** teacher, Miss Goodapple, with William T. C. Baumgarten.

"Oh, no!," moaned Horace.

"What luck," groaned Morris.

"Wait until roll call," suggested Luke. "Then we'll find out his real name."

"Good morning, class," chimed Miss Goodapple after showing **the** new boy to **the** vacant seat in **the** back of **the** room. "Let's see if we are all here."

"Horace Homecoming."

"Here."

"Chester Filbert."

"Here."

"Morris Townley."

"Here."

"Iris Fogel."

"Here."

"Luke Warner."

"Here."

"Fern Fiddlehead."

"Here."

The teacher called every name but **the** one Horace, Morris, and Luke were waiting for.

"Boys and girls," said Miss Goodapple. "I would like you to meet **a** new classmate."

Horace, Morris and Luke sat up straight.

"This is William T. C. Baumgarten. I hope you will make him welcome."

"Now we'll never find out," whispered Horace.

"Who cares," whispered Morris.

"There must be another way," whispered Luke, still thinking about **the** bicycle.

"Quiet, everyone," said Miss Goodapple, beginning **the** lesson. *"Today is October 14th, **the** day on which **the** battle of Hastings was fought in **the** year 1066. On that day William I won **the** crown of England and became one of **the** most powerful kings of **the** Middle Ages."*

Horace sat up and listened carefully. He liked stories about kings.

*"William was born more than nine hundred years ago in Normandy, which is now **a** part of France. His father, Robert **the** Devil, duke of Normandy, died on **a** pilgrimage. William, at **the** age of eight, became ruler of **the** Normans.*

*"Some of **the** Norman nobles didn't want **the** young boy to be their ruler. After three of William's guardians were murdered, **the** child was kept in hiding until he was old enough to protect himself and his dukedom.*

*"William grew into **a** strong youth and **a** bold warrior. By **the** age of twenty he had defeated many of his enemies and held strong control over Normandy."*

Luke sat up and listened carefully. He liked stories about warriors.

"**The** king of England at this time, Edward **the** Confessor, was William's cousin. He had promised that William would succeed him to **the** throne of England. However, when Edward **the** Confessor died, Harold, Earl of Wessex, not William, was named King.

"William was furious. He should be King of England, and king of England he would be! He threatened Harold with an invasion. He vowed that he and his army would cross **the** sea, and that he, William, would take his rightful position on **the** throne.

"King Harold gathered together an army and waited on **the** southern coast of England for William's ships to appear. They waited and waited. They waited all summer. Finally, when autumn came and William had not appeared, Harold disbanded **the** army. **The** soldiers returned home to harvest **the** crops.

"At that moment, who should appear in **the** north with an army? Not William, but someone else who wanted **the** throne of England. **The** King of Norway!

"Harold raced to **the** north, gathered together another army, and after **a** difficult battle, defeated **the** Norwegian king. It would have been **a** great victory for Harold, but that was **the** very moment William had been waiting for. While King Harold was driving **the** Norwegians out of northern England, William and his troops crossed **the** sea and landed in **the** south.

The king quickly received *the* news of William's landing on *the* coast of England. King Harold marched south; William marched north. They met on *the* battlefield called Hastings."

"A long hard battle raged. From nine in *the* morning to six at night William's army tried again and again to break through Harold's lines, with no success. Finally, William brought his weary troops together once more and this time charged straight through *the* middle of Harold's line. William had won! Harold was killed in battle. *The* defeated army was scattered.

"William marched on to London. On Christmas day in *the* year 1066 he was crowned William I of England. Today we know him as William *the* Conqueror."

Morris sat up straight in his seat. "William **the** Conqueror," he repeated to himself. "William T. C. Baumgarten. William **The** C. Baumgarten." Morris leaned over, tapped Luke on **the** shoulder, and whispered, "William **The** C. Baumgarten."

"William *the* Conqueror, as king of England, proved to be *a* strong and efficient ruler," continued Miss Goodapple. "He improved *the* law courts..."

Luke wasn't listening to Miss Goodapple now. He leaned over to tap Horace on **the** shoulder and whispered, "William **The** C. Baumgarten!"

Horace, Morris, and Luke looked at one another and together whispered, "William **The C.** Baumgarten." They spun around to look at **the** new boy.

*"One of the lasting monuments of William **the** Conqueror's reign is known as **the** Domesday Book. It consists of **a** long listing..."*

Horace looked at William **The** C. Baumgarten and smiled.

*"...of **the** entire land of England, including **a** count of **the** number of tenants, **the** number of plows, **the** numbers of forests, **the** number of fish ponds...,"* went on Miss Goodapple.

Morris looked at William **The** C. Baumgarten and smiled.

And Miss Goodapple went on, *"...not an ox or **a** cow or **a** pig was left out of **the** listings in **the** Domesday Book."*

Luke looked at William **The** C. Baumgarten and smiled.

*"And that is **the** story of William **the** Conqueror,"* finished Miss Goodapple.

William **The** Conqueror Baumgarten, his head held high, turned toward Horace, Morris and Luke. William **The** Conqueror Baumgarten smiled back at his new friends.

THE END

Ellen **The** Author Raskin has also written *Nothing Ever Happens on My Block, Silly Songs and Sad, Spectacles, Ghost in a Four-Room Apartment* and *And It Rained*.

Ellen **The** Artist Raskin has illustrated many other books by various authors. She studied art at **the** University of Wisconsin and was an award—winning commercial artist before she began making children's books.

Ellen **The A.** Raskin was born in Milwaukee and now lives in New York City with her husband Dennis Flanagan and her daughter Susan.